OSA'S PRIDE

ANN GRIFALCONI

Little, Brown and Company

Boston   New York   Toronto   London

Also by Ann Grifalconi

The Village of Round and Square Houses

Darkness and the Butterfly

First Edition
Library of Congress Cataloging-in-Publication Data

Grifalconi, Ann.
   Osa's pride/Ann Grifalconi. — 1st ed.
      p.   cm.
   Summary: Osa's grandmother tells her a tale about the sin of
pride and helps Osa gain a better perspective on what things are
important.
   ISBN 0-316-32865-0
   [1. Africa — Fiction. 2. Conduct of life — Fiction.] I. Title.
PZ7.G88130s 1990
[E] — dc19   88-28828
                                                             CIP
                                                             AC

               10 9 8 7 6

                        BP
        Published simultaneously in Canada
   by Little, Brown & Company (Canada) Limited

      Printed in the United States of America

Dedicated to
my brother, John, and Mia and Carl

When I was no bigger than a coffee bush
I learned something amazing about myself
That had to do with broken eggs, blue cloth,
And foolish pride!

As far back as I can remember
I have always lived with my mother and brothers
On my grandmother's coffee farm
Where Gran'ma says we grow the finest coffee in Africa!
Just across the way, lives my Gran'pa Omo,
Also my Uncle Domo,
Who claims *he* grows the finest corn
In the whole, wide world!

But I barely remember my father
For when I was still very, very small
My father was called up to fight in the big war —
And he never came home again . . .
My mother would never look at another man
And continued to live in Gran'ma Tika's round house.

Some said Mama was stubborn.
But Gran'ma understood her ways
And wisely let her be.
And so we all lived together happily
. . . Except for me!

You see, I too was very, very stubborn!
Though I was only seven,
I would believe nothing I had not seen.
So when I was told my Papa was not coming back
I refused to believe them.
"How do you know — for sure?"
They were silent, then.

From that moment on,
I became full of foolish pride . . .
For I believed that
If I closed my mind,
I could keep anything I did not like
From coming true!
And on the other hand — if I made believe,
I could make everything turn out the way I liked!

So I began to make up stories about my Papa.
I remembered that he had come from the big city
Long ago, and married my mother.
I imagined he was different from anyone else
Therefore he must be special and better!
And, since he went to war and never came back,
He must be a HERO, too!
That made him *twice* as special!

Soon, since he was not there
To tell me it was not so . . .
I began telling all the other children
How wonderful my father was — so brave and so tall!

Now at first, they listened and agreed:
But when I spoke only of *my* father
And forgot to listen to *their* stories
About *their* parents
They soon began to leave me alone.

I made believe I did not care
And let them know that when *I* grew up
I would go away from this little village
And be educated at the University in the big city,
And — just like my papa —
I might decide never to come back, either!

My Gran'ma let me be for a while
Watching me carry my pride about,
Listening to nobody, head in the air . . .

But Uncle Domo, seeing me playing all alone,
Came over and crouched down to ask me
"Where are all your friends, Osa?"
"I don't need them!" I sniffed.
Uncle Domo shook his head.
Just then, Gran'ma called me over to her side.
"Osa! Come help me with this. I need your advice!"
Well, *NO ONE* had ever asked my advice before!

So I ran across the earthen yard
Where my brothers had raked out the coffee beans
To dry in the sun —
Over to where Gran'ma sat sewing
On a low stool in the cool shade by her house.
Uncle followed, too, after a while.
Spreading out the big blue cloth she was working on
For me to see, Gran'ma smiled sweetly.

I was very curious
For the women of Tos have a special skill:
They can make picture-stories
Out of little colored scraps of cloth
Which are sewn onto a long blue cloth.
This can be worn like a cloak or a skirt
Or sometimes, if it is very fine,
It is hung up to be admired and wondered at.

"What is the story this one tells, Gran'ma?" I asked.
Gran'ma patted the ground next to her.
"Sit by my side and I will show you."
She pointed to the sewn-on figure of a girl:
The girl seemed to be walking on a long line like a road
That ran across the middle of the cloth.
"You see that little girl?
She is on the road to market to sell her eggs."
I looked hard and said,
"But Gran'ma! The basket on her head —
It is *too* full of eggs!"

Gran'ma nodded.
"This girl is very vain and proud.
She thinks people are always admiring her!
She walks along with her head stuck up so high
That the eggs begin to fall out!"

I laughed so hard at the whole idea
I rolled over on my side!
But when Gran'ma unrolled the design
To show me what happened next,
I saw that Vain Girl walked right on!
And the eggs kept falling out behind her!
"Why doesn't she stop, Gran'ma . . .
And pack the eggs tighter?"

Gran'ma smiled slyly:
"Vain Girl makes believe she does not care
About all the attention she is getting.
She is so full of pride she *won't* look back!"

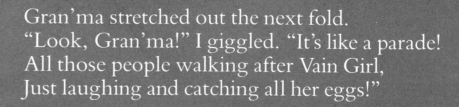

Gran'ma stretched out the next fold.
"Look, Gran'ma!" I giggled. "It's like a parade!
All those people walking after Vain Girl,
Just laughing and catching all her eggs!"

"Yes!" laughed Gran'ma,
"*She* thinks they are following her
Because she is so beautiful —
But *they* see only the trail of broken eggs behind her
And think she is foolish!"

"What will happen to her, Gran'ma?" I asked,
For I saw that the rest of the cloth was blank.
Gran'ma smiled, "You tell me, Osa . . .
What color shall I make her, then?"
"Well, when she gets to market
And finds she has no eggs left,
She will be so *mad* . . .
Maybe you should make her *purple!* . . .

No! When she finds out
That was why all those people were looking at her . . .
She will be so *embarrassed*
You should make her *red!*"

Gran'ma Tika leaned toward me.
"What do you think she will learn from this?"
I looked up at her wise old eyes.
"She will know . . . that her stubborn *pride*
Made her blind . . . to the truth."
Then, as I thought about that,
As Gran'ma knew I would . . .

I put down my head to let out my own tears of pride.
And Gran'ma hugged me 'til I smiled again.
Gran'ma's eyes crinkled as she looked down at me.
"If we could only see ourselves, Osa!
We would all be so much happier!"

That evening, when Gran'pa asked me
As he asked every night: "What did you learn today?"
I took a deep breath and said, very fast,

"I learned about broken eggs 'n foolish pride 'n . . ."
I looked over at Uncle Domo, who winked.
"I learned I'm no *better* than anyone else . . ."

And then I finished, surprising even him:
". . . But I'm no *worse*, either!"
And I danced off
To help Mama bring the supper in!

E   Grifalconi, Ann
GRI
           Osa's pride

$15.45

NOV 29 '95	DATE		
MAY 1 6 '97			